# Bootsi

## *number 2*

M

James, Mike

Bootsie number 2

JF

1945297

Text copyright © Mike James 2010
Published by Vivid Publishing
P.O. Box 948, Fremantle
Western Australia 6959
www.vividpublishing.com.au

# Chapters

# 1

See you Stinkey

"Are you sure you've got everything before we leave?," Bootsie's mum asked. "I sure hope so," replied Bootsie. "Well it's a long way to come back if you've forgotten something," his dad continued. "I've made sure I've got everything, I even double and triple checked," his sister added. "Ok then kids, lets all have one last look at the house before we leave," said Bootsie's mum as she put her hands on Bootsie's and his sister's shoulders.

The family stood as a group on the footpath and looked towards the house that had been the family home for the last 12 years. "I sure am going to miss this place," said Bootsie's dad. "Yes, it's been a good home," replied his mum. "Do we really have to leave, Dad?" questioned Bootsie as he looked up at the large SOLD sticker on the FOR SALE sign outside the now empty house. "It's a bit late now tiger, the house has been sold," his dad replied. "Besides you might even like it where were going. It sure is closer to the beach," he added. "But what about my friends at the club and school?" said Bootsie as his eyes started to become teary. "C'mon son, we've been through this before, you and your sister will make new friends at your new school and I'm sure they play rugby up there," said his dad as he tried to cheer Bootsie up. "But I like it here, Dad," Bootsie pleaded. "How do you know you won't like it in the new place?" his dad questioned. "Let's give it a try at least, you might even like it. I've been given a great chance within the company and I think it's going to be great up there for all of us, otherwise I wouldn't have taken the new job," his dad added as he walked Bootsie and his sister over to the car.

"We'll follow you up there," said Bootsie's dad to the driver of the removal truck. "Sure thing, once we get there it'll be pretty late so we'll find somewhere to park the truck near to your house. We'll be right to sleep in the truck and meet you at the house in the morning" he replied. The removal truck started its engine, and the footpath was soon covered in clouds of thick black smoke.

"Quick everyone in the car, it's time to go," said Bootsie's dad. Bootsie rolled down his window as they slowly drove away from the house. He leaned out of the window and started to wave. "Goodbye house," he said. As they got to the end of his street, he saw Stinkey Taylor sitting on his bike talking to some other boys and girls. "Goodbye Stinkey," Bootsie shouted, as he waved to Stinkey. "Hey Bootsie," Stinkey shouted and began pedaling after the car. "See you Stinkey," Bootsie shouted, as Stinkey got even closer.

"Take care, Bootsie," Stinkey shouted, as the car began to pull away. Bootsie continued to look back at Stinkey as he tried his hardest to keep up with his dad's car. "See you Stinkey," Bootsie whispered to himself as he watched Stinkey eventually disappear from his view.

On the way out of his town, Bootsie asked his dad if they could drive past the South's Bulldogs clubhouse for the last time. "I've got to follow the truck son," his dad replied. "If he goes that way then we'll drive past it, but it depends on which way he goes," he continued. Fortunately for Bootsie he did get to drive past and see the clubhouse for the last time. "See you clubhouse," he said to himself. "See you posts," he continued. "See you grass," he added. "Ok Bootsie, I'm sure there will be grass and posts at your new club," his dad interrupted.

"I know, but not these posts and this grass," Bootsie replied. "I've played here since I was six years old, all my friends are here and Coach Van Den," Bootsie said to his dad. "This is where I won my first grand final trophy," Bootsie continued. "How do you know you won't win one at the new club?" his dad asked. "What if the coach isn't as good as Coach Van Den?" Bootsie replied. "What if he is?" replied his dad.

"Speaking of trophies did you remember to put it in your suitcase?" asked Bootsie's mum. "Err, I think I did," replied Bootsie, as he scratched his head trying to remember putting in the bag. "What if I forgot it, can we come back and get it?" he asked. "Not for a while," his dad replied. "You'll just have to win another one with your new club," his mum said as she turned around and smiled at Bootsie. "I doubled checked, it was in there, don't worry," continued his mum. "I wouldn't let you forget that, I know how much you treasure it. You slept with it for the first three weeks after you won it," she said to him as she handed him a bag of lollies. "Here, share these with your sister. We've got a long trip ahead of us."

His mum was right, the family did have a long trip ahead of them. Bootsie's dad had been given a new job in his company and it meant the family had to move far away from where Bootsie was born and grown up. Bootsie turned around and watched the South's Bulldogs home ground disappear into the distance out of the back window of the car.

So many thoughts went through Bootsie's head as they drove for what seemed like forever. What will my new school be like? Do they have a rugby team there? Do they even play rugby there? If they do what is the team called? What will the other players be like? Will they even like me? Bootsie could feel his heart start racing. What if they don't like me? What if they don't pass me the ball? What if I can't play as good as I do for the Bulldogs? What if the coach won't give me a game?

All the worrying he had been doing in the car and the very long trip must have made Bootsie tired, because he soon drifted off to sleep. As the car pulled into a driveway of a house, Bootsie started to wake up. He looked over at his sister who was still fast asleep. "Where are we?" Bootsie asked as he looked out into the dark night. "We're here," replied his dad. "Already?" said Bootsie. "What do you mean already, you two have been asleep for most of the trip," his dad laughed. "It's dark outside," said Bootsie. "It sure is," replied his dad. "We'll just make do for tonight and unpack everything tomorrow," his dad continued. "Where will we sleep?" Bootsie asked. "The sleeping bags are in the boot of the car, we'll use them tonight, it'll be like camping," his dad replied. Bootsie went inside the new house and had a quick look around. "Well, what do you think?" asked his mum. "It's big, really big," he replied.

Bootsie's mum knelt down next to him as he rolled out his sleeping bag. "This move means a lot to your dad, it's a very good job for him so I want you to really try and enjoy living here, ok? It's going to be a big change for all of us, not just you," his mum said. "I know, Mum," replied Bootsie. As he slid into his sleeping bag, Bootsie looked up at the ceiling. A hundred questions went through his mind. He knew tomorrow was the start of a whole new beginning; he was excited and nervous about it all at the same time.

# 2

# High Ball

Bootsie woke up earlier than usual the following morning. The hard floor hadn't made the night's sleep easy. Anyway, it felt really strange waking up in a new house knowing this was now where he lived. "Why don't you go and ride your bike around a bit and see what the new town is like," said Bootsie's mum as she rolled up her sleeping bag. "Are you sure that's ok?" he replied. "It's fine, the removal men will be here soon and I don't want you getting under their feet," his mum answered.

Bootsie went outside. Just as he pulled his bike off the bike rack on the back of the car, the removal truck arrived. He was soon surrounded by a cloud of black smoke. "Oops, sorry about that," said the removal man as he jumped down from his truck. "She's a good old girl, just blows a bit of smoke," he jokingly continued. "Mum and dad awake are they?" he asked

Bootsie. "Um, yeah I think so," replied Bootsie, as he tried to ride away from the smoke. "Just ring the bell," he shouted as he rode away from the house.

Bootsie rode to the end of the street, had a quick look and rode straight back to the removal truck. It sure was a strange feeling not knowing where he was, or how to even get to his school. For the rest of the morning he continued to ride to the end of the street and back, not daring to venture any further. He watched the removal men heave and strain as they carried all the furniture from the old house out of the truck and into the new house.

He went back inside the house around lunchtime for a bite to eat. "Wow," he said to his mum. "It looks strange with most of the furniture in here now," Bootsie added. "It's starting to feel like home," his mum replied. Bootsie ran into his new bedroom, his dad had placed his suitcase on his bed. He quickly unzipped it, to search for his grand final trophy. "Aagh, there it is," he said as he picked it up. He read the engraving on the trophy out aloud, "Under 11's grand final winners." He thought about all the other players in the South's Bulldogs and wondered what they were doing now. He placed the trophy on his desk in the same spot it had been in his old house, had a quick look around the house and went back out to the removal truck.

As Bootsie watched the removal men continue to unload the truck he heard a voice shout, "High ball!" coming from somewhere further up the street. "Who was that?" he asked the removal man. "I don't know," the man replied. "Only one way to find that out, young fellow," the removal man continued. "How?" Bootsie replied. "Go and have a look, silly," the removal man joked. "Oh, yeah, of course," replied Bootsie as he picked up his bike. He slowly rode up to where he thought the voice came from. "High ball!" he heard someone shout again. He looked around but could not see any-one. "Drop goal!" he heard someone shout. As he looked up, a rugby ball came flying over the roof of a house in his street and bounced along the grass onto the front lawn of the house towards where Bootsie was riding.

The ball slowly bounced into the front tyre of Bootsie's bike and stopped rolling. He got off his bike and laid it on the front lawn of the house from where the ball had come. As he picked the ball up, he saw a boy come running from the side of the house towards him. The boy was jumping in the air and was commentating as he ran along. "Yes, and young Robbie kicks the winning drop goal and wins the World Cup for his team and his country, what a superstar!" The boy looked up and saw Bootsie holding his ball. "Yes, the losing team looks very sad," the boy said as he ran over to Bootsie. "Yes, the winning captain gets given the game ball by the losing captain," continued the boy as he took the ball from Bootsie. "A great win. They wouldn't have been able to do it without him," he continued, as he ran back down the side of the house and out of view, without saying a word to Bootsie.

"What a strange kid," Bootsie said to himself as he stood next to his bike, wondering what had just happened. "High ball!" he heard the boy shout from behind the house, as he watched the ball fly up in the air and disappear again, as it came down and out of Bootsie's view. "Drop goal!" he heard him shout again. Once again the ball flew over the top of the house and bounced towards him, landing near his bike. The boy came running from the side of the house, still continuing to commentate his every move. "Have you ever seen a player like this before?" he said to himself. "No, I don't think the world has seen a better player than Robbie before," he continued. "The losing team still hasn't left the field. They're probably still amazed at what a great player young Robbie is," he continued to say as he picked up the ball near Bootsie.

Once again he ran back down the side of the house and disappeared from view, still not having said anything to Bootsie. "This kid is crazy," Bootsie said to himself, as he picked up his bike and began to ride home again.

"High ball!" he heard the boy shout again as he rode off. "I hope all the kids here aren't mad like that," he thought to himself as he rode up next to the removal truck.

"Make a new friend, did ya?" asked the removal man as he closed the back of the truck. "What do you mean?" asked Bootsie. "High ball!" the removal man laughingly said. "Oh, him, what a weirdo he was," replied Bootsie. Bootsie's mum and dad came out from inside the house to say goodbye to the removal men. The removal men waved goodbye as they drove away, filling the street with clouds of black smoke. The family walked towards the curb as they watched the truck drive further up the street.

Bootsie looked up the street and could see the boy from before, holding his rugby ball under his arm and waving to the removal truck as it drove past his house. He also turned and watched the truck disappear as it turned the next corner. Just before Bootsie's family went back inside their new house, the boy turned around and waved to Bootsie and his family. "Who's that?" asked Bootsie's mum as she waved back to the boy. "I think his name's Robbie," Bootsie replied to his mum. "Is he a new friend you made today?" his mum asked back, exited that Bootsie might have made a new friend already. "No mum, I sort of met him before, but that is one strange kid," replied Bootsie. Bootsie and his family laughed as they walked back into the house ready to sleep in their own beds again, now that all the furniture had arrived.

# 3

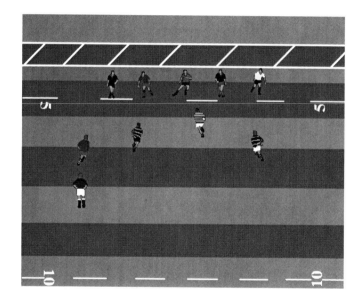

# Touch

'DING DONG,' went the doorbell the next morning. "Ooh our first visitor," Bootsie's mum said, as she got up from the breakfast table and headed towards the front door. Bootsie could hear his mum talking but couldn't hear who she was talking to. "Who do you reckon that is?" he asked his dad. "Only one way to find out," his dad replied.

Bootsie got up from the table and walked towards his mum, who was still talking to someone at the front door. "Yes that's my son," Bootsie heard his mum say to the other person. "Of course, I'm sure he would love to. I'll just go and ask him," his mum said as she turned around and saw Bootsie standing behind her. "Oh, here he is now," she said. "This lovely young boy wants to know if you want to go the park with him," his mum said to Bootsie with a big smile on her face.

As his mum stepped aside, Bootsie could see who she was talking to. "The name's Robbie," the boy at the door said, as he put out his hand for a handshake. "Bootsie," replied Bootsie. "Robbie was wondering if you wanted to go to the park with him and meet some of his friends," Bootsie's mum said again.

"Just a quick game," Robbie said as he threw his rugby ball in the air and caught it again. "A quick game of what?" asked Bootsie praying he was going to say rugby. "Of touch," replied Robbie. Bootsie stood still. "Touch rugby," Robbie said trying to excite Bootsie. "Oh, cool," Bootsie replied, "Can I go Mum?" Bootsie asked. "Of course you can, just come home around lunchtime to eat," his mum replied back.

Bootsie picked up his bike and began riding alongside Robbie. "New in town are you?" asked Robbie. "Yes we got here yesterday," replied Bootsie. "I saw the removal truck yesterday and hoped the new family in the street had kids," Robbie continued as they rode along together. "Have you got any brothers or sisters?" Robbie asked. "Only a sister but she's younger," replied Bootsie. "No brothers?" Robbie asked again. "Nope, just a sister," Bootsie replied. "I haven't got any brothers or sisters, I'm an only child," said Robbie. "My mum reckons I'm enough to handle, whatever that means," continued Robbie.

"Do you like rugby?" Robbie asked. "Are you kidding? I love it" replied a very excited Bootsie. "I saw you yesterday kicking the ball over the roof of your house," Bootsie said to Robbie. "Why didn't you throw me the ball then?" asked Robbie. "What do you mean?" Bootsie replied. "When I kicked it over the first time and you picked it up, you just held onto it like it was a baby and you were scared of dropping it," said Robbie. "I just thought you didn't know what a rugby ball was," he added. "Are you kidding me?" Bootsie replied. "I was just wondering what you were talking about," Bootsie added. "I was winning the World Cup," said Robbie. "Do you know what the World Cup is?" Robbie asked. "Of course I do," replied Bootsie. "I love rugby," he added.

"My team won the grand final last year," Bootsie said proudly. Robbie pulled on the brakes on his bike and he stopped suddenly. "What did you say?" Robbie asked. Bootsie also stopped his bike, "I said, my team won the under 11's grand final last year," Bootsie replied. "Which team?" asked Robbie. "The South's Bulldogs," replied Bootsie brimming with pride. "Never heard of them," said Robbie as he began to ride of again. Bootsie tried to catch up to him, "South's Bulldogs, we beat the Western Rebels in the final and I scored the try that won the game," Bootsie continued as he rode alongside Robbie. "That was where I used to live, but," Bootsie said with a hint of sadness in his voice.

"Do you play? For a team I mean," asked Bootsie excitedly. "Sure do," replied Robbie. "Rugby Robbie they call me, I love the game," Robbie continued. "I've never played in a grand final, but. Last year we didn't even make the quarter finals," Robbie added. "Oh, great," Bootsie said to himself. "Are there many teams around here?" asked Bootsie. "Are you kidding? It's like a religion around here," Robbie replied to a now very happy Bootsie. "That's why we're playing touch today. To get ready for the new season," said Robbie. "Do you need any more players in your team?" asked Bootsie. "Please, please say yes," he thought to himself. "I suppose so," replied Robbie. "Let's see how you go playing touch first, but," said Robbie.

Bootsie was so excited when they arrived at the park. Robbie rode over to a group of boys waiting nearby. "You said 9 o'clock," one of the boys said to Robbie. "Yeah, yeah I was showing the new boy around," replied Robbie. "Boys this is Bootsie, he's new," said Robbie. "Can he play?" one of the boys asked. "Reckons he scored the winning try in the grand final last year," replied Robbie. "OOOOH," all the boys said as one. "That was where I used to live," Bootsie said to the boys. "Well you better be good if you want to play for our team," one of the boys snapped. "Shut up, ferret," Robbie snapped back, "We didn't even make the quarter finals last year, remember?" Robbie added. "Now let's get this game underway," he continued.

Bootsie was so excited to know how popular rugby was, around where he was now living. He had played many games of touch rugby before, during the off-season, and during training sessions with the Bulldogs. He soon showed Robbie and the other boys that he could play. "Man these boys are good," Bootsie thought to himself. "I can't believe they only made the quarter finals. I can't wait until the real season training begins to see what I'm really in for."

"You're not bad," Robbie said to Bootsie, as he drank from his water bottle. "Thanks," replied Bootsie. "You guys are really sharp," Bootsie continued. "Oh, that's not even our first team. Some of these boys just keep the bench warm," replied Robbie.

Bootsie was shocked and worried, "If some of these boys sit on the bench, what's the rest of the team like then?" he asked Robbie. "I guess you'll find out on Wednesday at the seasons first training run," replied Robbie. "That's if you want to come down," he added. "I wouldn't miss it for anything," replied an excited Bootsie.

# 4

# Devastated

Bootsie was so excited when he got home from his new school on Wednesday, he could hardly stop talking. "What's up with you?" his mum asked. "Don't you remember? It's my first night's training with the new team," he replied. "Oh, has the season come around already?" his mum asked. "Yep, and tonight's the first training session," replied Bootsie. "When does Dad get home?" he asked his mum. "Not till late, on Wednesdays," she replied. "How will I get to training?" he asked. "I'm sorry but I can't take you, I've got too much to do around here," his mum replied. "Can't you ride your bike there?" his mum asked. "I suppose, but it's a long way," Bootsie replied. "Well it's your only real option if you want to go," his mum added. "How does Robbie get there?" she asked. "Oh, he goes to someone else's house after school and they go together with that boy's dad,"

Bootsie responded. "Guess the bike it is then, I'm afraid," his mum replied. "Sorry son, but we've only got one car at the moment, and your dad has to work late on Wednesday's with his new job," she added. "It's ok, Mum, I'll ride. I just want to get there, that's all," Bootsie added. "Got to make a good impression on the new coach," he continued.

Bootsie soon left for training. He had ridden to training on his bike plenty of times with the Bulldogs, but the South's Bulldogs ground wasn't very far away from his old house. The closest rugby club to his new house was a lot further for Bootsie to ride to, and plus to make matters worse, the road to the new rugby club was very hilly and some of the hills were huge. Four times, Bootsie had to get off his bike and push it, to get to the top. He was starting to get used to his new town and knew where the oval was. He arrived just as Robbie and the others were warming up. Robbie ran over to Bootsie as he arrived. "Are you Ok?" Robbie asked. "You're really red in the face," he added. "I'm stuffed," gasped Bootsie, "It's all uphill," he added. "Lots of hills around here," replied Robbie. "C'mon, I'll introduce you to the coach."

"Isn't that?" Bootsie said. "Yep, it sure is," replied Robbie. "Didn't he play seventy test matches?" whispered Bootsie, as they got closer. "Seventy-seven," replied Robbie. "Why is he the coach?" asked Bootsie. "His daughter plays," replied Robbie. "His daughter!!" shouted Bootsie. Upon hearing Bootsie shout, the coach turned around and looked at the boys, he was a big man. "Err, Coach, this is Bootsie, he's new in town," Robbie said to his coach. Pl .. pl... ple..

pleased to meet you, Mister," Bootsie stammered. "Just call me Coach, Ok?" the big man replied. "Have you ever played before?" he asked Bootsie. "Yeah, for sure," replied Bootsie. "Well get out there, let's see what you've got," he asked. "If you're half as good as Robbie, you'll be doing ok," he continued.

Bootsie trained hard for the first fifteen minutes, but the bike ride up the hills to training had really taken it out of him. His legs felt like jelly as he tried to keep up with the other boys. Every time a play was made, Bootsie was fifteen metres behind it. He didn't seem to be making a good impression on the coach or his teammates at all. He was shocked by how good some of the other players were, especially Robbie. Bootsie thought some of the South's Bulldogs were good, until today. "This team would have smashed us last year, and they only made the quarter finals," Bootsie said to himself as he tried to keep up with the play. "What are the teams that made the quarter finals like?" he wondered. "Ok, take a break," the coach shouted to the players after about forty minutes or so. Bootsie was more pleased than anyone to take a rest. He was stuffed!!

During the break the coach came over to Bootsie. "Where did you play before?" he asked Bootsie. "For the South's Bulldogs, down South," he replied. "But my dad got a new job and we moved here over summer," Bootsie added, still trying to catch his breath. "Oh, I see, well if you want to make the team here you're going to need to keep up with the play," his new coach said to him. "It's just, I'm a bit.." Bootsie tried to get his words out over his heavy breathing. "Ok, no excuses, just do what you have to do to keep up with the rest of the players if you want to make the team," his coach added. "Alright, that's enough. Back out on the field you go," the coach shouted to the players who were still resting. Bootsie was devastated; he was the star player for the Bulldogs. Coach Van Den had never told him he wouldn't make the team before. "It's not my fault I had to ride my bike here and this place is so hilly," Bootsie thought to himself, as again he tried to keep up with the play.

He was determined to make a good first impression but it had failed. After training had finished he waved goodbye to Robbie as he picked up his bike to go home and started to walk his bike across the field. Robbie was standing with a group of boys and one of them shouted to Bootsie "Winning try in the grand final, Hah! You can't even keep up." Bootsie was so upset, he wanted to go over to the boy and stand up for himself. He could feel the tears in his eyes starting to build and knew that if he went over there he might start to cry. He was so disappointed how the first training run had gone. He just continued to walk his bike across the oval away from the group.

The only good thing about riding up hills is that when you go the other way it's all downhill. Lucky for Bootsie, his legs were very sore and tired from riding to training in the first place, and then trying to keep up all evening. He was very sad as he rode home. He thought to himself "That's it, I'll just quit. I don't want to play for this stupid team anyway. I'll go back to the Bulldogs, at least Coach Van Den knew I could play well." Deep down, Bootsie knew this was not going to happen and the South's Bulldogs were a long way away from where he now lived.

As he got home, his dad was sitting out the front of the house drinking a beer. "How did it go?" he asked. "Terrible, thanks to you," Bootsie snapped. "Hey!" his dad said. "There's no need for that," he added. Bootsie burst into tears. "I'm s..,, sorry Dad," he cried, as he hugged his dad. "I hate this team. I want to go back to the Bulldogs and Coach Van Den," he sobbed. "C'mon son," his dad said, as he hugged Bootsie. "You can't let one bad night get the better of you. Where's your fighting spirit?" his dad asked, now with a wet shirt from Bootsie's tears. "I just wanted to make a good impression and I didn't," he continued as he tried to dry his tears. "Next time. You'll get 'em next time," his dad replied. "The race is long and it's all about who wins in the end, ok?" his dad continued. "Now go inside, have a shower and something to eat, get a good night's sleep and you'll feel a lot

# 5

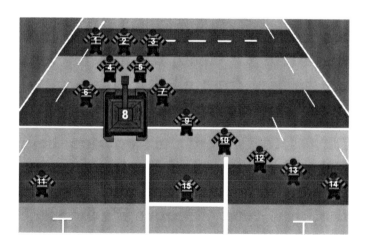

# Tank

When Bootsie woke the next morning he lay in bed and thought, "Today is a new day, I'll just forget about last night and move forward from today." He tried to lift his legs out of bed. "Ouch!!" he said to himself. "My legs are killing me from riding up those hills last night." He slowly made his way down the stairs to breakfast, one step at a time. "Oh, dear, are you ok?" his mum asked, as he hobbled into the kitchen. "Yeah, it's just my legs are so sore from all the hills around here," Bootsie replied.

DING DONG, went the front door bell. "I'll get it!" shouted Bootsie's sister, as she flew past him and towards the front door. "Bootsie it's for you," she shouted. Bootsie got up from the table and hobbled to the front door. "Hey Bootsie," smiled Robbie, "Are you ok?" he asked. "I hope that's not from last nights training run?" asked Robbie. "Nah, it's from the ride to training. All those hills, you know," replied Bootsie. "Yeah, there are some killer hills around here," laughed Robbie. "Do you want to come for a run before school?" asked Robbie. "No thanks," replied Bootsie. "I can hardly walk, let alone run," added Bootsie. "No problems, just thought I'd ask anyway," replied Robbie. "Oh, and don't worry about what that boy said last night, you know, the winning try comment. I'm sure it was just a joke, they're a good bunch when you get to know them," continued Robbie. "Nah, it didn't bother me one bit," said Bootsie, knowing it was a lie. "Ok, see you at school then," said Robbie as he ran off up the street towards the other waiting boys.

Bootsie hobbled around the house with sore legs until Monday, when the pain slowly started to go away. He kicked the ball around in his back garden on Tuesday night, but he still couldn't feel his legs properly and didn't stay out for long. The following afternoon when he got home from school, he was hoping to see his dad's car in the driveway, but it wasn't. "Where's Dad?" he asked his mum, already knowing the answer. "You know he works late on Wednesdays now, it will be every Wednesday from now on. If he could change it, I'm sure he would. He wants to make a good impression on his new boss just like you do with your new coach," his mum told Bootsie. "Yeah I know I was just hoping not to have to ride again," Bootsie sighed. "Chin up," said his mum, as she waved him goodbye.

Bootsie made his way to training on his bike again. Some of the hills seemed even bigger this week. His legs were still sore from his ride last week. This week he had to get off and push his bike up *five* hills to get to the top. He arrived at training in worse condition than the previous week. He rode over to the coach, "Hello Coach," he said. "You're back," was all his coach said in return. "Well don't just stand there, out you go," his coach added. Bootsie walked out towards the other players who were already warming up. "Hey Bootsie," said Robbie. "Glad you made it," he continued. "The grand final hero is back for more punishment, is he?" said one of the boys. Bootsie just sucked in a deep breath. "I'll show you," he said quietly to himself.

"Ok you lot, bring it in here," called the coach. "Ok, the season starts in two weeks. We've got tonight and next Wednesday to choose a team. So if you want to play, you've got to train, and by that, I mean whoever I see putting in the effort will get a game, understand?" continued the coach. "Now, you know roughly where each of you wants to play, so split up into the forwards and the backs. Bootsie, where do you normally play?" the coach asked Bootsie. "Usually number 8," he replied. "All the boys started to laugh," "You've got no chance," said one of them, as they continued to laugh. "He's trying to take your spot," one of the other boys said, as they all looked over at one of the other boys standing in the forwards group. "No chance," the boy said, as he glared at Bootsie. "Let's see how you go with the backs first, hey," said his coach. "The backs," Bootsie thought to himself.

The forwards moved to one side of the field and the backs moved to the other side. Bootsie started playing on the wing when he first started, but as he got older and bigger he was always placed in the forwards. "This is going to be different," he said to himself as he took his position in the backline.

From the opening play, Bootsie was a mile behind the play, his legs were so sore he could hardly run, let alone get anywhere near the ball. Every time the ball got fed out, Bootsie was twenty metres behind and he never got near the ball once. Some of these boys were so fast that Bootsie wondered if Red and Ted would even be able to keep up with them. Legs was one of the boys who played on the left wing and a boy they called Flash played on the right wing. Boy, were they fast! Robbie was sensational, he was number 10 and played fly half. His kicking was sensational, Bootsie didn't like to say it but he was just as good, if not better than the 'Super Boot' Ben Smith, back at the Bulldogs. Bootsie had never seen 'Super Boot' drop kick the ball over his house before. "Take a break," shouted the coach. "Bootsie was exhausted and wondered if he would make it through the rest of the evening.

The coach pulled Bootsie to one side at the break. "Have a run with the forwards in the next bit, ok? We'll see if you fit in there better, don't worry, we'll find you a spot. As I said before, it's all about trying and I can see you are really trying out there," his coach smiled as he walked away. "But I.., it's just that..," Bootsie tried to speak to him and tell him about the hills and the bike. "Ah, c'mon no excuses, just do what it takes to get on the team remember?" the coach added, as he continued to walk over to the forwards. Bootsie slowly walked over and joined them as well. "Ok, this is Bootsie, he's usually number 8 but let's see how he goes with you lot," the coach said to the rest of the forwards.

"Let's set up two scrums, Bootsie you can be number 8 on one of them and Tank you're number 8 on the other one, we'll see who's got the goods," the coach instructed. Bootsie looked over at the other number 8, the boy they called Tank. He was very solid and had massive legs.

The scrum was set and the ball came out under Tank's feet, Bootsie's legs were like jelly and he felt like he couldn't push the scrum from behind at all. Tank picked up the ball off the back of the scrum and ran forwards. One of the flankers on Bootsie's scrum peeled off and tried to tackle him. Tank just palmed him off like a fly and kept running. Bootsie broke away from behind the scrum and thought this was a great chance to impress the coach. It didn't work. He got smashed. Tank ran straight over him and he was picking grass out from his teeth for ages. "Great work," shouted the coach. "That's why she gets a game every week, she's got heart!!"

Bootsie wasn't sure if Tank had knocked him a little bit silly. "Did he just say she!?" Bootsie asked the flanker as they both picked themselves up after just being flattened by Tank . "Yep, that's Tank, the coach's daughter. She can only play for this season. Girls can't play in this competition until they're seniors. There aren't enough girls to make up a full junior girls competition. Well actually, she's the only one anyway," the boy continued. "You'll *never* get the 8 jumper while *she's* playing," he continued to say to Bootsie. "I'm Ferret, anyway," the boy said to Bootsie. "Yeah, we met playing touch the other week, I live near Robbie," Bootsie added. "Oh, schoolboy Robbie over there, I thought I'd. seen you before," said Ferret. "What does schoolboy Robbie mean?" asked Bootsie. "If you're any good around here, you'll get picked to play in the schoolboys' team for the Regional Cup or Shield. There's a team for each age group above this one. Robbie is a sure thing," continued Ferret.

Bootsie's legs were still sore as he tried to ride home, he couldn't run properly, couldn't keep up with the other boys in the team and now to make things worse, his favourite position was taken by a girl. He still hadn't asked what the team was even called. How worse could this get?

# 6

Caution
**HILLS**
Ahead

# Last Chance
# to Impress

All week Bootsie had thought about Tank. "Imagine if the boys from the South's Bulldogs knew that I couldn't play number 8 up here because a girl plays in that position, they would laugh at me," Bootsie said to himself. At least this week he had been able to run around in the back garden a bit more with his favourite rugby ball. It was great having Robbie in the street as well; Bootsie and Robbie would play either at Robbie's house or at Bootsie's house. Robbie commentated on each game and didn't stop commentating until they were called inside for dinner. "Ferret told me you would be playing schoolboys next year, is that true?" Bootsie asked Robbie. He continued to commentate as he ran around "Yes, he'll definitely get picked for the schoolboys team next year, the form he's been in, a certain future test player, this one. I don't think the country's ever seen a fly half anywhere near as good as young Robbie." As he commentated, he continually ran around the back garden sidestepping anything on the ground and throwing dummy passes to Bootsie. "And look at young Bootsie," he continued to commentate. "Can't get a game because he's getting smashed by a girl, but not just any girl, it's the coach's daughter Tank, great player, not so good on the looks however." Bootsie and Robbie broke into laughter. "She is good you know," said Robbie. "You might have to look at another position, for this season at least. She can't play next year which is a shame because in action, she's awesome," continued Robbie. "It's no shame if you don't play number 8, the coach will find you another spot you'll see," added Robbie. "I don't think he likes me," replied Bootsie. "He keeps saying no excuses, just do what it takes to make the team, in his booming voice," added Bootsie. "You'll see, you'll see," Robbie replied. "Hey, what's the team even called?" asked Bootsie. "Northern Hornets," replied Robbie. "You know what a hornet is?" asked Robbie. It's like a bee or a wasp, except bigger and angrier, just like the Tank." Robbie laughed as he started to buzz around the garden like an angry hornet.

Bootsie rode to training again the following Wednesday afternoon. He was amazed to make it nearly the whole way without stopping on any hills to push. His legs were still sore but as he rode he noticed some new muscles in his legs, which had never been there before. He was quietly impressed. He arrived at training and rode over to the coach. "Hello Bootsie, back again I see, and not so red in the face this week. Getting a bit fitter riding up all those hills on the way to training I imagine," his coach said. "How do you know?" asked Bootsie. "Because we drive past you every week and we see you struggling up the hills as we drive past," his coach added. My daughter was pretty impressed with the tackle you tried on her last week, she said," he continued. "But she ran over the top of me," Bootsie replied. "Bootsie, she runs over the top of everyone that's why we call her the Tank. She said to me you nearly stopped her and she doesn't say that too often. Now off you go and join the others."

Bootsie was surprised to keep up a bit more at training this week, he still lagged behind a bit but for the first time he managed to keep up and got his hands on the ball and made some good runs. A few times he heard his coach shout "Good, Bootsie, good." Tank came over to him during the break and said hello. "Are you the boy that won the grand final last

year somewhere?" she asked Bootsie.
"Yeah, I played for the South's Bulldogs
before we moved here in the summer,"
replied Bootsie. "Have you heard of
the South's Bulldogs?" he asked her.
"No, never," she replied. "It seems like
a dream to even think of them now,"
said Bootsie to her. "Did you win a trophy?" she asked. "Yes, a good one," he
replied. "Well it wasn't a dream then,"
she added. "I'm Bootsie," he said as
he went to shake her hand. Some of
the boys looked and laughed as they
saw the two of them shaking hands.
"Don't worry about them," she added,
"My real name's.." she went to speak.
"Come on you two, get back to it," her
dad the coach shouted. "What's your
name?" Bootsie asked as they ran towards the others. "Just call me Tank,
everyone else does," she replied.

Bootsie stayed with the forwards for
the rest of the training run, he felt

good playing in the forwards he knew he was never going to be fast enough to be a back. He started to get to know his teammates a bit better as well and started to get to know their names, which was a lot easier when calling for the ball to be passed to him when he got near it, anyway. During the last minutes of the evening's training, one of the backs whose nickname is Scruff (because his hair looks like it has never been brushed in his life), came charging down the centre towards Bootsie. Bootsie put an amazing tackle on him and Scruff lost the ball completely. Bootsie looked up to see the coach with a slight grin on his face. At the end of the evening the coach never mentioned it to him and he wondered if he had even seen it. He knew it would be hard to get into this team, but he hadn't realized just how hard it would be. There were some great players in this area; Bootsie was looking forward to the game on Saturday just to see what some of the other teams in the area were like.

At the end of the evening, the coach called all the players into one group. "Ok, Saturday is our first game of the season, now I've seen some good things from all of you so far. Those who continue the hard work will be rewarded with a game. Look around you, each player is your teammate, but you have to continue to try and try hard and I promise you that you will get a game. It's all about heart, and who's got one. It's up to you to show me just how big your heart is." "Wow," Bootsie thought to himself. "Do coaches go to school to learn these speeches; he sounds just like Coach Van Den before a game." His coach continued, "Saturday, meet at the ground nice and early, for the jumpers to be given out. I'll make my decision over the next few nights about which players will be playing where. If you don't get a game don't get upset, just keep showing effort at training. You will be rewarded, I can't tell you this enough, now go home and rest."

Bootsie rode home wondering if he would even get a game on Saturday. For the first time since he had started playing at six years old, he had never wondered if he would get a game on Saturday before. He knew this competition was a lot harder than he had played in before. He also knew the players in his team were a lot better than he had played against before, as well. It was going to be tough, but as he rode home and looked down at his new leg-muscles pushing his pedals around, he also knew that with hard work anything was possible. He remembered Coach Van Den's advice to the Bulldogs last season. All year

# 7

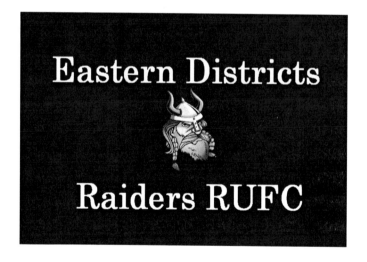

Eastern Districts
Raiders RUFC

## Round 1

It was Saturday morning and Bootsie wasn't excited at all. For the first time since his mum had laced up his first boot when he was six years old, the first game of the season was usually one of the happiest days of Bootsie's year. Even his mum noticed as soon as he sat down at the table, "Bacon and eggs," she said with a smile, knowing he would never turn them down before a game. "I don't care." replied Bootsie. His mum was shocked, Bootsie had never been so unhappy before the first game of the season. She definitely knew something was wrong when he wasn't bothered if he had bacon and eggs or not. "Isn't today the first game of the new season?" she asked. "Yes, but I won't be playing," he replied. "What do you mean you won't be playing?" asked his surprised mum. "The players here are so much better than where we used to live. There are so many players at the club and it seems like every boy around here plays rugby," replied Bootsie. "Oh, I see," she replied, "First you were worried that they didn't play rugby up here and now you're sad because everyone plays, is that right?" she questioned. "No, I'm glad they play up here but the competition's so much harder. I am not a star player here like I was at the Bulldogs," Bootsie sighed. "Oh, Bootsie," she said, "You've just got to show them you *are* a star," she added. "But I'm *not*, mum, not here anyway," he answered. "Well you're a star to me," she said as she put a plate full of bacon and eggs in front of him.

"Mum!" Bootsie shouted from upstairs after finishing his breakfast. "Where are my new black shorts for rugby?" he asked. "On top of your chest of drawers, there should be a pair of black and amber socks on top of them," she replied. His mum came up the stairs and into his room, "Look," said Bootsie as he showed his mum that he couldn't get his legs through the bottom of the shorts properly. "My legs have grown," he smiled. "They sure have, I only bought them a month ago," his mum replied. "Look at the muscles in your legs," she gasped. "That's from all the hills on the way to training," Bootsie explained. "Well they'll have to do for today, that's all you've got and we haven't got time before the game to get you another pair," she added. "Doesn't matter, I won't be playing anyway," replied Bootsie. "Not with that attitude you won't, anyway," said his mum, with a frown on her face.

Bootsie arrived at the ground with his parents and sister, quite early before the game started. He couldn't believe how many kids were at the ground, there were hundreds and hundreds of them. The first game was a home game and it was a lot easier getting to the ground in the car, his legs weren't tired at all when he arrived. When he looked around the ground, he noticed all the other kids wearing black shorts with black and amber striped socks like he had on. Some of the younger grades were already playing games and Bootsie noticed the Northern Hornets club jumpers were exactly the same as the Bulldogs jumpers except they were black and amber stripes with some small red striping on them as well. "Wow, look how many kids are here," his dad gasped. "I told you, everyone around here plays," Bootsie replied. "So you won't laugh at me if I don't get to play?" he asked his dad. "What? Of course not, Bootsie," his dad replied, sounding shocked by Bootsie's last question.

Bootsie and his family walked around the ground until Bootsie saw his coach and his daughter watching a game that was already in progress. Bootsie walked over with his family and said hello to the coach. "Hey Coach," he said, "Hello Bootsie," he replied. "Hey Bootsie," said Tank who was standing next to her dad. "My little brother is playing in this team," she added. "Which one is he?" asked Bootsie. "See the one sitting down over there pulling the grass out of the ground, that's him," she replied. "Doesn't like the game really," said his coach to Bootsie and his parents. "I've got one girl who loves the game and can't play after this year, and a boy who can play but wants to pull grass out of the ground instead of playing. Life sure is strange," he added.

One by one the rest of the team arrived and stood near where the coach was. "How many players have you got in one team?" Bootsie's dad asked Bootsie. "Heaps," he replied. "I don't think I'll ever get a game here," Bootsie added. The coach's son's game finished and Bootsie's game was next. The coach opened the bag of jumpers and started reading from a list. One by one he went through the jumper numbers starting at number 1 right through to the 15. The coach read out his list like this.

1. Loosehead prop, 'Brains'. Real name Brian: spelt it wrong on his own registration form.

2. Hooker, 'Matty'. Real name Mathew.

3. Tighthead prop, 'Big Arnie'. Real name Arnold.

4. Second row (lock forward), 'Dozer'. Real name Thomas: fell asleep in class once.

5. Second row (lock forward). 'Locky'. Real name Lachlan, stands next to 'Dozer'.

6. Blindside flanker, 'Ferret'. Real name Fred: brought his pet ferret to school once.

7. Openside flanker, 'Waves'. Real name Paul: loves surfing in summer.

8. Number 8, 'Tank'. Real name: (she won't tell anyone), built like a tank.

9. Scrum half (half back), 'Mouth'. Real name Tyrone: Has a problem with his big mouth that gets him into trouble a lot.

10. Fly half (First five-eighth), 'Rugby Robbie'. Real name Robbie: mad about rugby.

11. Left wing, 'Legs'. Real name Mike: strong legs great runner.

12. Inside centre (Second five-eighth), 'Scruff'. Real name Tiarie: Seriously this boy's hair

has never seen a comb or a brush.

13. Outside centre, 'Sidestep'. Real name Nonu: has a wicked sidestep.

14. Right wing, 'Flash'. Real name Ashley: runs past you in a flash.

15. Fullback, 'Mark'. Real name Mark: always calls for the mark when under pressure inside his 22.

Bootsie wasn't surprised when Tank got the number 8 jumper instead of him. He felt his dad's hand squeeze his shoulder gently when it was given to her. "Ok, reserve players," said the coach. "Reserve players, we never had reserve players for the Bulldogs, we were lucky to have fifteen show up," Bootsie thought to himself. The coach continued to read from his list.

16. Reserve hooker, 'Bootsie'. Real name: (Can't tell you yet).

17. Reserve prop, 'Horse'. Real name: Chris Horsewith.

18. Reserve second row, 'Victor too tall': Real name Victor (Very tall).

19. Reserve flanker, 'TJ'. Real name Trevor: busts into opposition fly halves.

20. Reserve scrum half, 'Jackie Boy'. Real name Jack: loves playing scrum half and cycling.

21. Reserve back, 'Flea'. Real name Flynn: isn't the biggest player in the world but plays with a big heart.

22. Reserve back, 'Backsie'. Real surname: Baxter.

"Ok that's the twenty-two players for today if you didn't get a jumper don't get upset, just keep coming to training and put in the effort. We've got fifteen minutes until kick off, so the players with jumpers can start warming up please," the coach instructed after the players had been given their jumpers. Bootsie was so pleased to be on the list, even if he was a reserve hooker. "How hard can it be, Stinkey used to do it with no problems, well, apart from the fact he couldn't throw straight in a line out," Bootsie said to his dad. "See, you didn't think you'd even get a game," his dad replied. "You must have impressed the coach in some way," his dad added.

Bootsie went on the field and warmed up with some of the forwards. Tank came up to him and said that her dad had seen the tackle Bootsie did on Scruff at training on Wednesday and liked what he had seen. The game soon started and for the first time, Bootsie watched it from the bench.

The team they were playing was called the Eastern Districts Raiders. Their club colours were all black just like the All Blacks and almost like the Western Rebels who at least had a little bit of white on their socks and shorts, this team's colour was all black. It was a strange feeling, watching, as he had never done this before; he was very keen to get out onto the field and play. The first half went by and he still hadn't been called off the bench to play. Matty, the first choice hooker was very good and put the ball in straight at every line out. Some of the other reserve players got to play in the game late into the second half but Bootsie spent the entire game on the bench watching. It was a close game against the Raiders who had made the semifinals last year, but today they beat the Hornets 21 to 14.

Bootsie felt quite sad on the trip home, sure he had been selected on the reserve bench but he still didn't get to play in the game. It was the first time he had ever watched his team from the bench. He knew he had to keep trying, if he really wanted to impress his coach and make the team. Bootsie wanted to be a Hornet and not one that just sat on the bench and watched.

# 8

*It's all about heart*

# It's All About Heart

Bootsie was up very early on Sunday morning and ran down to the smaller park near where he lived. He had plenty of energy inside him due to the fact that he hadn't played yesterday. He started by stretching his legs, which still hurt but nowhere near as bad as before. Anyway, "No pain no gain," he said to himself as he continued to warm up. Bootsie knew the only way to become a Hornet was to train and get faster and stronger. He could feel in his legs that all the riding he had done on the way to training had made his legs bigger and stronger. When he ran, he could feel an increase in his running speed and it made him feel good about himself. He started with two laps of the oval at a slow jog. Once he felt he was warmed up, he started to drop kick the ball away from him as far as he could and then he would jog out to get it, pick it up and sprint back to score a pretend try on the try line. He must have done this twenty or thirty times before he had to rest.

After a quick rest he walked over to the rugby posts, stood on the five metre line in front of the posts and threw the ball at the black dot which was in the middle of the crossbar. He threw it just like the hookers he had seen on TV do it. "Coach Van Den used to make Stinkey do this," he said to himself as he continually threw the ball. After about thirty throws he started to hit the black dot on the middle of the crossbar every time, he was very pleased with himself. Bootsie then started to kick the ball as high in the air as he could, he would run after it and try and catch it before it bounced in front of him. If he couldn't get to it or he dropped it, he made himself do twenty push ups and twenty sit ups as a punishment. It sure made him run faster and harder to catch the ball.

Bootsie went to the park every afternoon straight after school and did the same training routine he had done on Sunday morning. Robbie came down on Tuesday and the boys did one hundred metre sprint races against each other. Robbie won every race but Bootsie didn't mind, it just made him run faster. Wednesday afternoon came and Bootsie couldn't wait to get to training. He got home from school and noticed his dad's car was in the driveway. "Hey little buddy," his dad smiled to him as he walked in the door. "Why are you home so early?" Bootsie asked his dad. "I don't have to work late tonight, so I can drive you to training if you like," replied his dad. "No thanks I want to ride, its good training for my legs," Bootsie said to his dad. "Why don't you ride your bike with me, Dad?" Bootsie asked. "Oh, ok," his dad gulped, not really wanting to ride up all the big hills he was used to driving up in his car. "It will do you good," Bootsie's mum laughed as she patted Bootsie's dad on his ever-growing stomach.

Bootsie and his dad left for the rugby oval on their bikes. Bootsie was now used to the large hills and could power his way up to the top of them without stopping. His dad couldn't. "C'mon Dad, you'll make me late," Bootsie shouted as his dad tried to push his bike to the top of the first hill where Bootsie was waiting. "You go on ahead of me," his dad puffed, "I'll meet you there, I just need a rest," he added as he finally got to the top of the hill. "Ok Dad," said Bootsie, as he rode away, "This is the smallest hill that you have to get up Dad, they get bigger from here!" he shouted to his dad as he sped away. "Oh, great," replied his dad.

Bootsie arrived at training and rode over to the coach. "Hello Coach," said Bootsie. His coach turned around and looked at Bootsie. "Oh, hello Bootsie," he replied. "Has your dad made it yet? We saw him struggling up the hills behind you on the way here," coach added. "No I left him behind," replied Bootsie.

"Where is everyone?" asked Bootsie as he looked around and noticed only half the players were at training. "Happens every year," replied his coach. "After the first game I choose twenty two players and then the next Wednesday all the players who didn't get a game don't come to training anymore. No heart, no commitment," he went on to add. "If they came to training and put in the effort, they would get a game I would guarantee it. But it's the same every year, no heart you see. Commitment Bootsie, do you know what it means? It means when you start something, you've got to finish it. Commitment, remember that word, Bootsie," his coach added. "*I* didn't get a game," said Bootsie. "You will, you've obviously got heart and commitment, otherwise you wouldn't have come back," his coach replied.

The hills on the way to training and Bootsie's extra training at the park had helped his rugby training greatly, he felt fitter and stronger already. No longer was he getting left behind and struggling to keep up. Now he was starting to pull ahead from some of the other boys. They played an eleven-a-side game, with full tackling and five man scrums. The boy who had laughed at Bootsie on the first training night, about him not being able to keep up, grabbed an intercept pass and started to run towards the try line for what would have been an easy try. Bootsie turned around and chased after him, Bootsie could feel the new power in his legs and he caught the boy and tackled him from behind just before he would have scored. "Now that's heart and commitment," the coach shouted from the sideline. "Great work, Bootsie," he added. Bootsie was so pleased with his efforts; he couldn't wait to hear what his dad thought of the try-saving tackle. When Bootsie looked around he could see that his dad still hadn't made it to the ground yet. Bootsie played hooker in the scrums and really felt strong in his legs, his scrum could easily push the other scrum over, eventually his coach had to put his daughter Tank, in the back of the other scrum to make it more even. They did some lineout practice and Matty the starting hooker, showed Bootsie how to throw the ball correctly at a lineout. For the first time, Bootsie felt like he belonged to this team.

He said goodbye to his teammates at the end of training and slowly walked his bike around, looking for his dad. Finally he saw him pushing his bike up the last hill and onto the ground. Bootsie jumped on his bike and rode over to him. "Never again!" his dad said breathing very heavily. "There are some big hills on the way here, aren't there?" Bootsie chuckled. "Anyway they're all downhill on the way home," added Bootsie, as he started to ride away. "C'mon Dad," he shouted as he began to ride home. Bootsie looked back and saw his dad pushing his bike towards him. "I'll see you back there," his dad said to him. "I'll just have to have a rest first," he gasped as he sat down. The coach beeped his car horn as he drove past and saw Bootsie's dad sitting on the ground next to his bike. The coach and his daughter waved to Bootsie's dad as they started to make

# 9

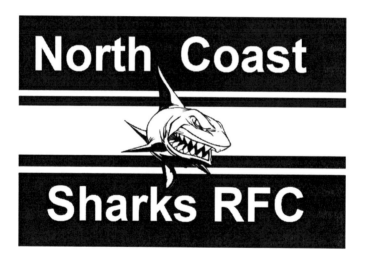

# Where's My List?

Bootsie rested on Thursday and Friday and didn't go to the park to do extra training. He wanted to be nice and refreshed for Saturday; he really hoped he would get to play this week. He really felt like he had come a long way from when he first arrived in his new town. He just had to look down at his very strong legs to prove it. His dad was still hobbling around the house after his bike ride on Wednesday and he moaned down every step on his way down the stairs to the breakfast table on Saturday morning. "Are you boys going to ride to the ground this week?" his mum asked with a cheeky grin on her face. "No!!" his dad quickly replied. They all laughed together, except his dad who didn't think it was funny at all.

It was just as well they didn't ride because Bootsie's next game was quite far away. The North Coast Sharks had a fierce reputation in this competition and had won the grand final two years ago; they were the real glamour club of the region. The team in Bootsie's age group had made it into the grand final last year but they were beaten by one point. North Coast had dark blue and white jumpers with a ferocious white pointer shark on the front of the jumper. Bootsie found his own team-mates after walking among a sea of boys in blue and white striped socks and getting some evil looks from most of them. "Friendly bunch up here," Bootsie said to his coach as he walked over and stood next to him. "Pretty proud club, this one," his coach added, "Fifteen test players have come from this club," he continued.

"Is everyone here yet?" the coach asked. "Yes there's twenty two players here, coach," replied Robbie. "When I read out your name and number just grab that jumper out of the bag and start to warm up over there," he said and pointed to an area nearby. The coach patted his pockets looking for his list. "I can't seem to find my list," he said to the players. "Oops," he added. He looked into the bag of jumpers and pulled out a piece of paper from inside the bag. "Ah, here it is," he said as he held the piece of paper in the air. He began to read, "That's last weeks team Dad," said Tank as the coach started to read from it. He had a good look at it, "Oh, yes, so it is," he replied. "Who was here last week?" he asked the group. Everyone put up their hands. "Ok then if you got a jumper last week put up your hand," he added. Once again, everyone put up a hand, "Easy then, whatever number you were last week you will be that again this week. Problem solved," he said as he screwed the piece of paper into a ball.

Once again Bootsie had to watch the game from the bench; he sat there and looked down at his new leg muscles, tightening them to make them look bigger. He couldn't stand the thought of not playing two weeks in a row, he had been training really hard and thought he had done what was needed to get onto the field, at least for one half of the game anyway. Bootsie got to see first hand why the Sharks were feared so much, by other clubs in this competition. They were big, strong, fit and fast boys. The game was very one sided in the first half and the score blew out to 28 to 0 by the end of the first half. The coach spoke to the players as a group at half time. "This is a good test of where we are this season; the Sharks are a quality team and will probably play in the finals again this season. If you want to know how well you have to play to get into the finals, it's time to show it now," he said to the team. "You have to be able to at least compete with them or they are going to walk all over you in the second half as well," he added. "Matty, I want you to sit off this half, Bootsie it's your time to show us what you can do," continued the coach. Bootsie was so pleased, "Finally he thought to himself."

Bootsie took the field with the rest of the Hornets' players. He took his position on the field and waited for the Sharks to kick off. The ball came towards where Bootsie was standing but was caught by Dozer. Dozer ran up field towards the Sharks defenders, with Bootsie running right behind him. Dozer ran straight into a wall of Sharks players and was tackled to the ground. He did well to protect the ball until Bootsie arrived and cleaned out the Sharks players, who were still on their feet trying to grab the ball. Bootsie continued to support like this for the rest of the half. The Hornets were playing some great rugby and Bootsie was in the thick of the action. Early into the second half, Bootsie had to pack down in his first scrum. He packed down in the middle of Brains and Horse who had also just come onto the field with Bootsie. Jackie Boy who had come on as the reserve scrum half, fed the ball into the scrum. Bootsie hooked the ball back and it worked its way back to the back of the scrum where Tank picked it up and charged over the line for a try. Robbie did a great kick and the score was now, Sharks 28, Hornets 7.

Bootsie was amazed he could keep up with the pace of the game. His strong legs helped him out in the scrums really well. He felt like he could really compete with the other scrum's front row. The Hornets scrum was rock solid and was a great match for the Sharks pack. Bootsie made some great tackles during the second half and really felt like he was helping his teammates. Bootsie was amazed to watch the coach's daughter, Tank, and how hard she could tackle. He thought to himself, "I don't think some of the Bulldogs' players would get up after being tackled by her." He continued to try his best in the second half and further impress his coach and teammates. Hooker was a new position for Bootsie, but he felt like he could really do well at it. Nonu was a great centre for the Hornets and put a lovely sidestep on a Sharks player to get over the line for another try to the Hornets. Unfortunately for Robbie, he got the ball down right next to the corner flag. It was still a try but it made the conversion kick a lot harder. Bootsie had never seen Super Boot get one over from so far out before, and thought that Robbie would struggle as well. He was wrong, Robbie stood and looked at the ball on the kicking tee for ages then he looked up at the posts, started his run up before the Sharks defenders charged at him. He was very relaxed and with the help of the wind the ball sailed high in the air, over the black dot on the cross-bar and gained the Hornets two more points. The referee blew his whistle and said, "That's the end of the game." Final score Sharks 28, Hornets 14. Bootsie's team hadn't won but they had held the Sharks scoreless in the second half.

"Great second half effort," Bootsie's coach said to the players as they walked off the field. Bootsie was exhausted; he had really tried his best to impress his coach. He felt pretty

# 10

Northern Hornets

Rugby Union Club

# Do What You
# Have to Do

Bootsie was very sore on Sunday morning after the game. It was certainly faster and harder than he was used to at the Bulldogs. He slowly walked his way down to the park for his Sunday morning training session. He started to stretch his aching body and tried to loosen up his sore spots. He went for a slow jog around the oval and slowly started to feel a bit better. The game had really taken it out of him and he was nowhere near as fast as he had been in previous sessions. He practiced his lineout throwing at the crossbar again, which were spot on. It only took him about ten throws to get the ball hitting the black dot. He did some drop outs where he drop kicked the ball out to the halfway line, jogged out to it and sprinted back to where he had kicked it from. His legs were pretty sore, so he only sprinted back at half pace. Robbie came down but only watched because he was also sore from the game. "You've come a long way since you first got here," said Robbie as he watched Bootsie train. "Yeah, I feel a lot fitter and stronger," Bootsie replied.

Robbie stayed for a little while before he returned home again. Bootsie was about to go home himself, when a man out walking his dog came over to speak to him. As the man approached, Bootsie realized it was his coach. "Hello Bootsie," he said as he got closer to Bootsie. "Oh, hello Coach," Bootsie replied. "I didn't know you lived around here," Bootsie said to him. "Yep, I live right over there in that house with the big brick wall out the front," his coach replied. "I've seen you down here training for the last couple of weeks. I also watched you push your bike up the hills on the way to training when you first came to town. I'm pleased to see that you have no trouble getting up them at all now," added his coach. "Yeah, it was tough at first, my legs.." Bootsie tried to tell his coach about his legs not being strong enough before. "Aagh, no excuses," his coach interrupted. "Do whatever it takes to make the team, remember?" added his coach.

Bootsie finally understood what the words meant, that he had heard the coach say many times to him. "Do whatever it takes to make the team," Bootsie replied back. "I have been," he added. "I know, I can see that by how much better a player you have become since you got here," said his coach. "Do you remember your first night at training?" the coach asked Bootsie. "Yes," Bootsie replied. "You thought you were a good player didn't you?" he asked Bootsie. "I thought I was," Bootsie replied. "If I had let you in the team straight away, would you have trained this hard knowing that you would get a game anyway? Let me answer that one for you, no! That's why I say to the players, do whatever it takes to make the team, I find out who's got heart and commitment straight away," he said to Bootsie. "But how did you know I wouldn't quit and not come back to training?" Bootsie asked his coach. "I didn't," he replied. "If you want to play at any top level in any sport or achieve anything in life, you have to have heart and commitment. If you do, you will be successful at whatever you try," continued his coach. "Bootsie, I played seventy seven test matches for my country and do you know how I got there?" he asked Bootsie. "Let me answer that one for you as well, I got there by doing whatever it took to make it into the team. No excuses, I just trained harder than everyone else around me. It paid off and I got selected, but that's when you've really got to have heart and commitment. Every player in the country wants that spot that you're playing in and you have to do whatever it takes to hang onto it."

"Do you understand what I mean?" he asked Bootsie. "Do you mean believe in yourself and you can do anything?" Bootsie replied to his coach's question. "Yes!" He smiled. "That's exactly what I mean, where did you hear that from?" his coach asked Bootsie. "My old coach used to say it, Coach Van Den was his name and he played seven test matches. He used to say it to our team last year," Bootsie replied. "Number Two's Van Den," Bootsie's new coach said as he roared with laughter. "What did you say?" Bootsie asked excitedly. "I think we're both talking about Yappy Van Den. He played some test matches before he got injured, good player too," his coach said. "Yappy Van Den," said Bootsie, "Coach Van Den's name is Yappy?" Bootsie asked. "Yes that was his name, Yappy Van Den. I got to know him very well on a tour once. They used to call him Number Two's Van Den, he was the starting hooker and apparently he nearly missed the start of a test match because he was so nervous and he couldn't get off the toilet. Is he coaching is he?" asked his coach. "Yes we won the grand final where I used to live last year," Bootsie replied. "Did you?" his coach said quite surprised. "He was a great player, a very fierce tackler if I re-member correctly," his coach added. Bootsie was still chuckling to himself, "I can't believe his name is Yappy, no wonder he made us always call him Coach Van Den."

Bootsie was so pleased to hear the story of Coach Van Den; he really missed his speeches before the game and at half time. His new coach was very similar to Coach Van Den, about the same age and size anyway. Bootsie's new coach was growing on him and he started to like him a lot more after what he had told him in the park. Not just about Coach Van Den but about doing whatever it takes to get into the team. The coach left Bootsie in the park to continue his training. Bootsie had really learned a lot from this morning's training run. He thought to himself about what the coach had said to him and how it had worked. He could have just quit and not gone back to training because it wasn't fair that he had to ride up some big hills to get there, or that the other boys got driven there and could run faster because their legs weren't tired. He could have even said that there are more players here and that's why I can't get a game. "Excuses, they're just excuses," he said to himself. "I'm such a better player now because of it," he continued.

At training on Wednesday, Bootsie put in more effort than he had ever put in before. He was so much fitter and stronger and he looked back at what he was like on the first night of training. He remembered how he couldn't ride his bike up even one of the smallest hills and now he didn't have to stop once. Even his dad couldn't do it. He remembered how he didn't touch the ball on the first night because he couldn't keep up with the other boys and how he nearly cried when one of the boys laughed at him about it. He had really worked hard, "I wish the Bulldogs' players could see me now," he thought to himself. He had come a long way since he first arrived, but there was still one hurdle he had to overcome, getting, and as his coach said to him in the park, keeping a spot in the first fifteen.

# 11

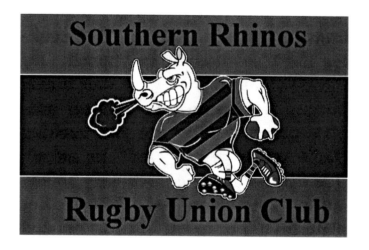

## "Bootsie Number 2"

Saturday morning, birds were singing outside Bootsie's bedroom window and the smell of bacon and eggs being cooked was in the air. Bootsie stayed in bed and let the smell from downstairs drift through his nose. "Aah, bacon and eggs," he said to himself. "Breakfast is ready!" his dad shouted from downstairs. "What's Dad cooking for?" he thought to himself. He ran downstairs to see his dad busily putting the bacon and eggs on people's plates. "Why are you cooking Dad? And where's Mum?" he asked. "It's our wedding anniversary today, Mum's staying in bed, I'll take her plate up to her to eat in bed," his dad replied. "Is she going to stay in bed all day?" he asked his dad. "If she wants to I suppose," he replied. "Isn't she going to come and watch me play?" Bootsie asked. "Yes," said his mum as she walked into the kitchen. "I was about to bring this up to you," his dad said to his mum. "It's ok, I'll eat it down here with you lot," she replied. "There's a bird outside my window that won't stop singing, how are you supposed to sleep in with that noise going on outside," she smiled to Bootsie.

"At least it's a home game again," Bootsie said to his parents as they drove to the ground. "We should have all ridden to the ground, you know, as a family," said his mum. "Sure, I'd be waiting at the top of the hills for you three to catch up all the time," Bootsie said from the back seat. "Oh, listen to Mr Tour De France in the backseat," his dad replied. "Yeah, sorry I forgot it took you the entire time I trained on Wednesday to even make it to the ground, Dad," Bootsie answered back. "I think I could ride up these hills without stopping for a break," said his mum. "No chance," his dad quickly replied. "Why don't we have a bet on it then," said his mum. "Ok, next home game we'll all ride here. Bootsie you can ride alongside your mum to see if she has to stop and push," his dad replied. "Ok, cool," said Bootsie, who now thought it was quite easy to ride to the ground. "Next home game it is then," his mum said finally.

Bootsie said goodbye to his parents who were still discussing who could and couldn't ride here without taking a break, and went looking for the coach. He finally found him watching his son pull grass out of the ground again as the rest of the players on his team ran past him to score a try. "Hello, Bootsie," his coach said. "Didn't see you down the park training for the last two days," he asked. "No, I always rest on Thursdays and Fridays," Bootsie replied. "Rest those legs hey, good idea," his coach continued. The rest of the players slowly arrived and gathered around the coach. "Where's my list?" the coach asked himself. "Please have another list than last week's one," Bootsie said to himself. "Aagh, here it is right where I put it," his coach replied to his own question. "Ok, number 1 at loosehead prop is Horse. Young Mr Horsewith came off the bench and played well last week. Reach in there and find the number 1 jumper son," his coach said. "Now, number 2, what have I written here? Bootsie, number 2. Where is he? Aah, yes, there you are, grab the number 2 jumper son, you deserve it. Number 3 is..". Bootsie stopped listening to the other names being read out. He was so pleased to have made it into the first fifteen. "Yes," he said to himself when he heard his name read out. He searched around for the number 2 jumper but couldn't find it in the bag. "Here Bootsie," Matty said to him as he handed the number 2 jumper to Bootsie. "I just thought it was mine," said Matty. "Sorry about that," Bootsie replied. "I just wanted a first fifteen jumper so bad I didn't even think it meant someone else missed out on it," Bootsie continued. "It's ok Bootsie, all the players have been talking about how hard you've been training and how much better you are now," replied Matty.

"Number sixteen, reserve hooker is Matty, where are you Matt?" the coach asked. "Here," said Matty. "On the bench today for the start of the game, ok?" coach said to Matty. "And for the rest of you I just want to say again, it's all about doing whatever it takes to make it *into* the team and once you're in there, *staying* in the team. If you want to know what this means, then ask young Bootsie over there. That boy has trained harder than any of you, not just at training but in his own time as well," his coach said to the group. All the players turned and looked at Bootsie; he tried to hide behind some of the other players but it was no good. "In fact Bootsie come over and stand next to me please," his coach asked. Bootsie made his way through the group and stood next to his coach. His coach was a huge man and Bootsie felt quite small standing next to him. "Have a look at this boy," he said to the group as he put his enormous hand on Bootsie's head. "Do you remember him at the start of the season? A little boy, who thought he was a grand final player and could walk straight into this team, well let me tell you now he is a grand final player and he has walked straight into this team. If the rest of you put as

Today the Hornets were playing the Southern Rhinos who had a red rhino as a mascot that ran along the sidelines for the entire game. Their club colours were red and black with a small white stripe. The game started at a cracking pace and Bootsie needed all of his extra fitness to keep up with the play. He charged into any rucks or mauls making sure he came in from behind the rearmost feet of the players in the rucks and mauls. He didn't want to give away any penalties for coming in from the side. There were a few scrums in the first half. With Bootsie up front, Horse and Brains on either side of him and Tank shoving from behind the scrum at number eight. It was unbeatable. At one point the Hornets' scrum pushed the Rhinos' scrum back over their goal line, after they had won a five-metre scrum. As soon as their scrum half fed the ball into the scrum, the Hornets' scrum pushed so hard, the ball ended up at Bootsie's feet. He quickly hooked the ball back and kept pushing and pushing. Pretty soon he saw the goal line go under his feet and he knew that when the ball crossed the goal line all Tank had to do, was place her hand on it and it would be a try. When he heard the referee blow his whistle and shout, "Try!" He knew it had worked a treat. With the successful conversion kick the Hornets were in front at half time. Hornets 7, Rhino's 0.

"Awesome job out there, so far," the coach said to the group at half time. You're finally working as a team and its showing. It was good to see the scrum win one against the head as well," he added. "Against the head, what does that mean?" asked Side-step. "When the ball gets fed into a scrum by the scrumhalf it goes in at his loosehead props' feet. He has his hooker standing next to him and they should win their own scrum. If their scrum gets pushed back and they lose the ball it's called, winning it against the head, by the other team. We have to start winning games, if any of you want to win a grand final trophy then doing things like that, is how you will win one," continued the coach, who didn't want to lose another game. The team gathered in a circle and all put their hands in the middle. "One, two, three, Hornets!" they shouted as one. Bootsie really felt like a Hornet now.

Bootsie loved his new position in the front of the scrum, he could really use his leg-power to push against the other team's front row and win the ball against the head. It happened to the Rhinos twice in the second half. Each time the ball was fed into the scrum,

Bootsie and the rest of the Hornets' forwards put on a great eight man shove to win back the ball from under the Rhinos' players' feet. It was great to watch and Bootsie's coach really let the Rhinos' mascot know what was happening.

Bootsie had done well in the lineouts as well, he had put the ball in straight to his lineout jumpers and they didn't lose a lineout all game. In one lineout Bootsie threw the ball to Brains who was standing in the front of the lineout. Brains reacted quickly and after he caught it, he threw it straight back to Bootsie. Bootsie took off towards the Rhinos' goal line; he had completely fooled the Rhinos' lineout players who were still back where the lineout had happened. It was up to the Rhinos' backs to catch Bootsie and stop him scoring his first try for the Hornets. Bootsie could see the backs charging towards him from inside their half. He was smart enough to head for the posts.

He remembered what Coach Van Den had said to the Bulldogs players last year. "You can't get pushed or tackled into touch, if you're nowhere near the touch line, so when you get the ball near the touch line start running infield towards your support players, not away from them." Bootsie remembered this and started to get away from near the touchline. As he got inside the Rhinos twenty-two, he was caught by a Rhinos defender who grabbed hold of his jumper and tried to pull him down. It didn't work, but it did slow Bootsie down enough for another Rhinos player to also grab hold of him. He pumped his legs and drove for the goal line. He realized this was what the extra training had done for him. He had two Rhinos players trying to pull him down and he was still on his feet and making ground. He made it to the try line just as Sidestep, Scruff, Flash, Waves and Ferret arrived from behind and drove him over the line.

The referee ran over to the massive pile of bodies on top of Bootsie. Pheew!! The referee blew his whistle. "Try!" he shouted. As the boys got off Bootsie and he got to his feet the referee said again. "Try. To that player number two." All the boys thought they had scored it. "Who's number two?" Ferret shouted. The coach's daughter Tank ran over and said "Bootsie scored it, Bootsie's number two." "Great try," she said to Bootsie. "Thanks Tank," he replied. "My real name's Becky," she whispered to him. "Oh," he said shocked that she had told only him her real name. "My real name's..." Bootsie went to tell her but she had already run back to the half way line.

Robbie did the rest and at the end of the game it was Hornets 14, Rhinos 0.

Bootsie had scored plenty of tries before, even the one that won the Bulldogs a grand final, but today's try was pretty sweet. He knew how far he had come in such a short time, all due to hard work. He continued to train extra hard both at training and down the park on his own or with Robbie. He could now match Robbie for speed and beat him in quite a few hundred-metre races. The extra training came in very handy, he held onto the number two jumper for the rest of the season, never once giving it back to Matty. Bootsie went on to score many tries for the Hornets that season. For the first time ever, they made the quarter-finals only to be knocked out by last year's grand final winners, the Central Cobras. It was also the last game that Becky played for the club. Next year she woudn't be allowed to play anymore, something about selection for the schoolboy squads and girls taking up boys' positions. Bootsie couldn't understand it, considering she was the only girl still left playing in the competition. Bootsie's coach couldn't understand it either and stopped coaching for the club when Becky had to stop playing. So next season Bootsie was going to have another new coach to impress. Robbie and Bootsie were also spotted by a regional schoolboy scout, who wrote both of their names down after the quarterfinal loss. Bootsie could feel big things were going to happen next season for him. He not only *felt* like a Hornet, he *was* a Hornet.

*The End.*

Check out the Bootsie website
www.bootsiebooks.com

Thanks to KooGa Rugby

www.kooga.com.au

Lightning Source UK Ltd.
Milton Keynes UK
UKOW05f1133291113

222083UK00005B/387/P